With love to Murray Horowitz,
the greatest sport I know
—A. K.

To Larry, Mo, and Squirrely
—D. C.

Margaret K. McElderry Books
An imprint of Simon & Schuster Children's Publishing Division
1230 Avenue of the Americas, New York, New York 10020
Text copyright © 2009 by Alan Katz
Illustrations copyright © 2009 by David Catrow
All rights reserved, including the right of reproduction in whole or in part in any form.
Book design by Sonia Chaghatzbanian
The text for this book is set in Kosmik.
The illustrations for this book are rendered in watercolors, colored pencil, and ink.
Manufactured in China
2 4 6 8 10 9 7 5 3
Library of Congress Cataloging-in-Publication Data
Katz, Alan.
Going, going, gone! : and other silly dilly sports songs / by Alan Katz and David Catrow.
— 1st ed.
p. cm.
Summary: Provides new, sports-themed lyrics to well-known songs, including "On Top of
the Bleachers" and "When Jimmy Gets in the Batter's Box."
ISBN-13: 978-1-4169-0696-4
ISBN-10: 1-4169-0696-7
1. Children's songs, English—United States—Texts. 2. Humorous songs—United States—
Texts. [1. Sports—Songs and music. 2. Humorous songs. 3. Songs.] I. Catrow, David, ill.
II. Title.
PZ8.3.K1275Go 2009
782.42—dc22
[E]
2007037798

Going, Going, GONE!

and other silly dilly sports songs

by **alan katz**   illustrated by **david catrow**

Margaret K. McElderry Books
New York   London   Toronto   Sydney

On Top of the Bleachers

(To the tune of "On Top of Old Smokey")

On top of the bleachers,
that's where we just sat.
Dad bought me a pennant,
a scorecard, and hat.

He got me some peanuts,
a soda, and chips,
a ballplayer puppet
that swings as he flips.

Next I got a helmet,
a bat, and a glove,
a giant foam finger
the crowd doesn't love.

Dad purchased a hot dog,
a cheese-filled dough puff,
an official backpack
to carry my stuff.

Twelve trips to the bathroom
Dad had to endure.
There mighta been a ball game . . .
though I'm really not sure.

Dad Took Me to Go Fishing

(To the tune of "Take Me Out to the Ball Game")

Dad took me to go fishing.
That's why we're on the lake.
Holding a rod with a hook and bait,
that's all you do—
you just sit there and wait.
Dad said fishing's really exciting
(I guess no one told the fish).
So we're gonna sit here all day.
Let's go home, I wish.

Not a bite in two hours.
Dad tells me to be still.
He says I chase the fish with my squirms.
Maybe they just aren't hungry for worms.
And we'll wait, wait, wait a bunch longer.
Until I'm sixty years old.
Though it seems all I'm gonna catch
is a rotten cold.

Finally Dad says we're finished.
Finally he says we're done.
He said he'd catch dinner, so he heads for
the fish department in our grocery store.
And the clerk threw Dad a large sea bass,
which he, of course, promptly bought.
So when Dad gets home, he can show Mom
the fish he caught!

I Gotta Make This Shot!

(To the tune of "Battle Hymn of the Republic")

My ball is near the hole
and my big shot is now at hand.
If I can sink this putt,
I'll be the greatest in the land.
Then they will put my name
on a new golf apparel brand.
I gotta make this shot!

I check my club, I check
the wind, I turn and face the crowd.
I ask them all to hush.
There's one kid who is really loud.
They'd better make him shush
so I can make them all so proud.
I gotta make this shot!

The pressure's on. My heart
goes thump. And then in no time flat,
I tap the ball and it
goes in! They all cheer, "How 'bout that!"
Compared to me, that guy
named Tiger is a kitty cat!
Because I made the shot!

Oh, the glory it's all mine now.
Everything is really fine now.
Gotta go get back in line now.
I sure love miniature golf!

The Great Skate Debate

(To the tune of "Polly Wolly Doodle")

Oh, we're gonna skate,
which is really great,
and I got a pair of skates that's really new.
Gotta plop 'em on,
and then whoosh—I'm gone!
Watch the figure-eights and twelves I'm gonna do!

First I lace.
Then I lace.
Then I lace pull pull pull lace.
Oops, the left is on the right, an'
gotta undo what I tightened.
I'll be there in just a minute, save me space!

Now the left's on right.
And the right's on tight.
'Cause at shoelace knots I'm really really grand.
So I'm set to go.
But a big uh-oh—
I can't skate in these 'cause I can't even stand!

Ankles turned.
I just learned
it is so much easier to walk than glide.
Both my skates, I will untie 'em.
Listen, do you wanna buy 'em?
I'll sip cocoa and just wait for you inside.

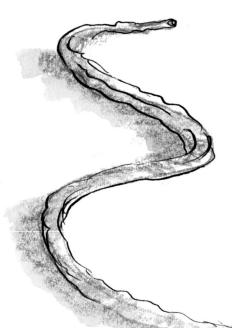

Ode to Umps and Refs

(To the tune of "Home on the Range")

In softball the umps
can be nothing but grumps.
As they yell,
and they tell
fair or foul.
And when they make the call
for a strike or a ball,
they don't speak in real words, they just growl.

Refs signal touchdowns,
and they say when you've stepped out of bounds.
Oh, they think they're so right
in their black and their white,
but their calls gave the blues to the Browns.

Yes, it's really a shame
that we lost the big game.
'Cause I screamed at the head referee.
I should've stayed calm.
(After all, it was Mom.)
Later, she'll blow the whistle on me!

Tennis Is a Complicated Sport

(To the tune of "Baa Baa Black Sheep")

Tennis is a complicated sport.
No one's guilty,
but it's *court*.
As for scoring, it
starts with *love*.
(But no kisses, one thing I'm glad of.)
Tennis is a complicated sport.
I'll say more, but please don't snort.

Tennis is a mystifying sport.
I have made a full report.
There is a *racket*,
but make noise, it's rude.
There is *serving*,
but no one brings you food.
Two opponents, yet it's called a *match*.
This game is a big head-scratch!

Tennis is an aggravating sport.
When I hit,
it's always short.
All my shots just hit the net.
I can't help but get upset.
I have learned a lot from Dad.
Mostly, words to scream when mad!

My Father Says We're Going Cycling

(To the tune of "My Bonnie Lies Over the Ocean")

My father says we're going cycling.
My mother says we're going far.
A family trip, whole day of bike-ling.
Why bother, when we have a car?

Pedaling.
Pedaling.
Way out of town past the seashore,
and more!
Pedaling.
Pedaling.
My brain and my rear will be sore!

My parents say it's recreation.
Dad tells me fresh air has its cost.
For him, that's a good explanation.
Where I sit, it's just car exhaust!

Cycling.
Cycling.
They pedal, I sit and I whine,
I whine.
Cycling.
Cycling.
A thunderstorm now would be fine.

All Fall Down

(To the tune of "Ring Around the Rosie")

Kickoff, the game's started!
Ouch, that tackle smarted!
Bashes! Bashes!
All fall down!

I am quarterbacking.
Other team's attacking.
Passes! Passes!
All fall down!

Now I try a sneak play!
But it is a weak play!
Smashes! Crashes!
All fall down!

Neither team is scoring.
For the fans, it's boring.
Gnashes! Mashes!
All fall down!

Though my body's swelling,
I am NFLing.
Football's such fun
all fall long!

I Need a Towel!

(To the tune of "Pop Goes the Weasel")

In the pool a second or two,
and Sue begins to howl.
H_2O, a drop in her eyes—
"I need a towel!"

Her eyes are wiped.
Sue goes back in.
She's such a waterfowl.
A splish!
A splash!
And then, oh no!
"I need a towel!"

Her nose, her lips.
Sue must wipe them off.
Her parents start to scowl.
'Cause each time they begin to sit down—
"I need a towel!"

Finally she is done for the day.
That's when Sue is upset—
the towel she needs to dry off
is soaking wet!

We're Choosing Up Sides

(To the tune of "The Wheels on the Bus")

We're choosing up sides for basketball!
Hope my name
they will call.
Compared to a flea,
I'm really tall.
Hope I get picked!

We started with ten and now there's eight.
There goes Fred.
There goes Kate.
Next chosen: my pet
Chihuahua, Nate.
Hope I get picked!

They're down to five, and then four, then three.
One question:
HOW 'BOUT ME?
A future all-star
and MVP.
Will I get picked?

The final pick and they call my name!
Hip-hooray!
Start the game!
They won't pass the ball,
but just the same—
glad I got picked!

Controlling Your Bowling

(To the tune of "Yankee Doodle")

Ten pins standing on the lane.
Look at me, I'm bowling.
Gonna knock 'em down with this
pink ball; here goes . . . I'm rolling!

I love bowling, every day.
Yes, this is where you'll find me.
Oops, the ball just slipped!
Hey, look out, everyone behind me!

Crash and smash the pins, such fun.
Yes, to me this is heaven.
Just got a strike on lane four!
(Though I'm on twenty-seven!)

I could be a pro someday,
though now I am confessin'—
the guy who owns the lanes just
paid me to take tennis lessons!

I Hope William Won't Tell

(To the tune of "The William Tell Overture")

Well, hello, got a bow
and a sharp arrow.
Archery will be fun
'cause I am pro.
I should charge lotsa bucks
just to watch my show.
Ready, set—okay, here we go!

Grab the bow, grip it tight,
and then pull it back
so the arrow can fly with a
mighty thwack!
Take a look and you'll soon see a
target smack.
Oh, no! Dad'll have a heart attack!

What a mess, oh such stress,
'cause my arrow fire
landed right in my folks' brand-new
sports car tire.
Yes, my miss
made it hiss!
Dad is filled with ire—
like the car, I think I'll now
retire!

I'm the Goalie!

(To the tune of "Oh! Susanna")

I'm standing in the netting
'cause the coach just put me here.
I'm totally alone.
Just what to do? I've no idea!

The other kids are way downfield.
Oh, please stay there, I beg.
The ball's untouched, they mostly
kick each other in the leg.

I'm the goalie!
Net is in my care.
Next week I should bring bug spray,
suntan lotion, and a chair.

The ball is loose, it bounds my way—
that's the last thing I need.
My teammates trip each other
as the other guys stampede!

I'm the goalie!
It's a five-on-one!
Is this what Mom meant when she said
that soccer is such fun?

What happened next I just can't say,
'cause I just closed my eyes.
They didn't score.
Now I have casts on both legs, to my thighs.

I'm the goalie!
And though it's not the same,
I finally enjoy soccer
on my new video game!

Going, Going, Gone!

(To the tune of "When Johnny Comes Marching Home Again")

When Jimmy gets in the batter's box—
Hurrah! Hurrah!—
he swings so hard that he knots his socks—
Hurrah! Hurrah!
The ball zips into the catcher's mitt.
Strike one! So Jimmy steps out to spit.
Then he steps back in.
The pitcher winds up and throws.

When Jimmy gets in the batter's box—
Three on! Two out!—
they're down by two and the team calls for a home-run clout!
Not likely, though; for the season he
is currently zero for ninety-three.
Still, the kids can dream as Jimmy stands in the box.

When Jimmy gets in the batter's box—
A curve! A curve!—
the kid unleashes a mighty swing
with all his nerve!
A line drive over the fence, like that . . .
unfortunately not the ball—the bat!
So it is strike two.
The pitcher winds up and snarls.

When Jimmy gets in the batter's box—
Grand slam! Grand slam!—
the stadium shakes with the sound of bat meets ball, bam-bam!
The people all got a thrilling lift!
Okay, I'm lying—the poor kid whiffed.
But at least he tried,
and wow, are you gullible!